# Shit Happens

## An Emotional Tale of Self-Empowerment and Self-Indulgence

**BY**

**Zoe S.**

# BEFORE YOU START READING, DOWNLOAD YOUR FREE DIGITAL ASSETS!

Be sure to visit the URL below on your computer or mobile device to access the free digital asset files that are included with your purchase of this book.

These digital assets will complement the material in the book and are referenced throughout the text.

## DOWNLOAD YOURS HERE:

www.AtomPublications.com

# Table of content

# Foreword

This book has been written with the intention of educating the readers about financial independence.

Before we start, I invite you to an imaginary world where you can choose to be either a 22-year old young man or a 23-year old young woman, so you can understand and enjoy this story even more.
The plot hovers over a young couple who falls in love in their early twenties. The story spirals out of control as Andrew repeatedly refuses to grow up and take life seriously.

Starting their love life with great joy and excitement, the couple finds their personalities clashing. While Kate is a responsible mature woman focused on her career Andrew is a wild spirit who never takes anything to heart.

Despite Kate's constant efforts to make Andrew realize not to throw his life away, Andrew was adamant on lying around and wasting his time. He drowns Kate in an ocean of emotions every time she manages to reach up to the surface.

One needs to take care of himself before he can take care of somebody else. Andrew learns his lesson the hard way when he hits rock bottom and is dispensed at the mercy of the others even for surviving.

Love is a beautiful feeling and should be cherished with a big heart but if it gets in the way of self-development and mature mindset, it can ruin lives.

# Chapter 1: Showered with May Love

"Come on. Come on, where is it?" Kate mumbled as she frantically tossed her shirts from the cupboard. "Maa! Maa! Have you seen my favorite white shirt?" she yelled, running downstairs.

A woman in her 70's was sitting on the couch watching television and petting a cat purring in her lap. The dark-faced Siamese jumped on the rug spooked by Kate sprinting down the stairs and scuttled out of the cat door.

"Kate! look you scared Dustie away," Rose sighed.

"Maa, I cannot find my white shirt. I laid it out on my bed this morning. I'm going to be so late. It's already four. Damn Josh would not let me end my shift," Kate let out her frustration.

"Calm down kid. It is in the laundry. I washed it," replied Rose.

"Oh maa! It was already clean," Kate dashed away.

"Not after Dustie's poo. It was not," mumbled Rose giggling.

All dressed up for her interview at a big firm, Kate caught the subway. The subway was fairly less crowded for a Monday evening. She kept checking her files nervously while the train stopped at the next station, and a group of boys just as young as her came aboard drenched by the rain. "Oh no! I forgot my umbrella," she mumbled, frustrated with her hand on her head.

A tall, fairly handsome boy wearing ripped jeans, a floral shirt, and sneakers caught her attention. He had a carefree spark in his eyes and a ravishing aura around him. He had an umbrella in his hand but was still soaked wet. The young man noticed her looking at him and walked towards her with a smile. Kate adjusted her files nervously and looked away. He stood near her, holding a pole. "Do not worry about it. You got it," he expressed to Kate.

"Excuse me?" Kate turned and looked at him, startled.

"I take it its first day? expressed the stranger smiling. "Or maybe…it's your interview."

"Yeah, it is," replied Kate and looked away.

"I wish you get that job," the boy shouted on the noisy train.

"Oh yes? Why are you so concerned with what that?" asked Kate.

"Because if you get the job I can see those pretty eyes every day," smiled the boy confidently with his sparkly eyes.

"Oh! Right!" chuckled Kate, "Good to know there are three people praying for my job now."

"I take it the third person is your boyfriend?" asked the boy.

"Actually no. My grandma," she replied, smiling.

"Why such a pretty and presumably smart girl judging by these pile of files not have a boyfriend?" flirted the boy, "Are you possessed or something?"

"Yeah I am the human Annabelle," giggled Kate.

The doors opened at the next station, and someone stomped on her shoe. When she looked up, the doors closed, and he was waving behind the glass, yelling, "Get that job!" His friends pulled him away.

Kate chuckled. She never really had any serious relationships. She never really felt something to excite her and warm her heart. She had a tickling feeling in her stomach that she had never had before, but at that time, she thought of it as nothing more than that, just a tickling feeling.

Days passed, and the happy subway seat remained empty. The minutes on Kate's clock were so well calculated for between her odd job and studies that she hardly had any time to think about anything else. She was a New York baby born out of a young couple still striving to figure out their dreams. Her parents separated just when she was two, and her grandmother took her in. Since then, "Maa" was the only parent she ever knew. Kate's tiny hands were always wrapped around maa's finger as a kid. As Rose began to lose her strength over the years, Kate grew to reverse those roles. Rose went along with her, but in her heart, she knew Kate needed her now more than ever. She was stepping out of the warmth of Rose's hug into the blue. She was still a little girl to her with so much hope and goodness in her big bright eyes against the wide strange world.

Kate hurriedly entered home and stomped on the mat to clean her muddy shoes. "Oh come here honey. There is still a lot of May ahead," Rose came out of the kitchen with a ladle in her hand. "May? More like dismay!" Kate said sarcastically.

"Now what are you doing with that spoon?" asked Kate and walked towards her worriedly.

"Oo it's nothing. I was making your favorite pumpkin soup. I knew you would be grumpy. It had rained a lot today," replied Rose stirring the pot.

"Maa, how many times I've told you to leave everything to me. You should not be in the kitchen," Kate put her head on Rose's shoulder.

"You do not tell me what to do, Okay? Do not boss me around. Now get the chair over here. You must be starving," replied Rose.

"What's with the long face, dear?" asked Rose as they sat with their tummies full and hearts not so much, "Worrying about that job, are we?"

"Yeah…it's almost been a month. They were going to get back to me in two weeks," replied Kate.

"You'll get it. Do not worry about it. I believe in you," soothed Rose.

"This waitressing job is tiring me. Josh gets really unreasonable with me. He is so rude," complained Kate.

"Come here, dear. It's gonna be okay. You are going to get that job," Rose put Kate's head on her chest and run her fingers through Kate's hair. "Who knows there might even be a handsome young man?" chuckled Rose, "Hmm? It might add a little excitement in your life?"

"Grandmaa! It is already enough exciting. Okay stop it," giggled Kate.

"Oh is that blushing I see? Are you blushing? Is there someone you are not telling me about?" eyed Rose.

"No! There is no one…" giggled Kate.

"Oh there is! Tell me. Tell me," replied Rose.

"It is nothing okay? But there was a stranger on the subway on the day of my interview who wished me to get the job so that he would see me every day," expressed Kate.

"Hmm. Is he handsome?" asked Rose.

"Mhm. He thinks I have pretty eyes," replied Kate getting up and smiling.

"Oh yes you do honey pie," replied Rose.

That day Kate could not sleep very well. One would think that the thunderstorm was the culprit, but Kate had seen too many of those to intrude her peace. The real culprit was her job interview. Thinking what she should have and should not have said, her exhausted body put itself in remission. The tree outside her window had given refuge to a caterpillar in its cocoon. As she dozed away, a beautiful yellow butterfly spread her wings and flew away, a soldier avoiding cloud bullets. The next day had something similar planned for Kate; another chapter to be added to her life story.

"Kate come downstairs quickly," shouted Rose excitedly. "What?" Kate came down, tying her hair, "I have my class." Kate mumbled curiously. Rose handed her the phone. Kate clang to the telephone like a kid to his last candy allowance of the day. "Yayy!!" yelled Kate and Rose. "You got the job!" exclaimed Rose, dancing.

"They said that they had lost my cell phone number. It took them so much time to find me here," Kate joined Rose.

The next day sun woke Kate with lots of happiness. She wore a blue shirt with a white skirt to match the sky. Just when she was about to leave with her umbrella, she stopped for a minute and put the umbrella back smiling. Her big eyes searched left and right for someone whom she had hoped to be there. The subway seemed crowded with faceless figures because he was not there. Finally, the train hissed to remind her what the day had to offer her. This day had made her one step closer to the life she had wanted, and so she confidently marched towards it.

May bid farewell and June brought its tender, warm breeze. Dustie, her cat was finally able to lie down in the grass, soaking the sun. June had waned Kate's need for the umbrella just like for the subway stranger who had found himself lost somewhere in the frantic life of the 23-year-old Kate. The sun woke her up with the role of a business trainee. The afternoon breeze wrapped her up in the role of a waitress. The chilly evening shook her with the role of a diligent student. The warmth of Rose's hug at night finally put the role-playing at a pause, or so did Rose think, but Kate was busy chasing stars even in her dreams.

On the tenth of June, nature decided to play a trick. It was warm and sunny until it was suddenly not. The sky missed the clouds, so it called out to them, and they responded with the same affection. In a minute, clusters of thick dark clouds embraced the sky. Kate was walking a block away from the subway station back from her job when the clouds lit up in all their glory, and the wind danced in joy. Kate drew her umbrella like a soldier in war, but the wind gushed and flew it away. Kate ran after it trying to catch it. The wind blew her hair in her face, and when she pulled them away. She saw a man holding her umbrella.

"Am I your umbrella guardian now?" expressed the stranger. It took Kate a minute to recognize the man, but the sparkle in his eyes against the dark evening gave him away. It was him. Kate chuckled, "What are you doing here?" "Seems like I was summoned by the higher powers to hand over the queen her umbrella," the stranger bent down on his knees with the umbrella smiling.

Kate laughed, picking up the umbrella, "Get up…! So what is my guardian's name?" "Umbrella guardian. Do not get carried away!" he laughed, "I am Andrew Tales and you are?"

"Kate. Kate Noah," replied Kate.

"Kate would you let your umbrella guardian have the honor of taking you for a drink?" Andrew smiled, walking with her.

"Right now?" asked Kate surprised.

"Yeah. Let's get in some shade. I know a bar right across the street," replied Andrew charmingly.

Kate and Andrew spent the next two hours chit-chatting and laughing. Andrew had sensed Kate's nervousness and blew it all away with his charm. The rushing endorphins in her body flushed her face with a glow. His honey pool eyes looked hypnotic in the red lights. One could just get drown in them if left too long staring at them. He was from the Drag, and it seemed like he had the whole Drag summed up in his personality. He had all the funk of the Drag. Andrew's body warped with colors, patterns, and jewelry would not stop talking about the genres of music he listened to every day.

"I feel like I have been talking too much. Tell me a bit about yourself. What do you like? What do you do besides your job which you got because of my good luck wish?" expressed Andrew nervously. It was odd and he had never felt nervous in front of a girl before, but maybe that was it. She did not come off as a girl. She came off as a woman who knew what she wanted, who she was, and who she wanted to be. He had dated women like him before, carefree and riding with the flow, but this woman could take the reins of an ocean in her hands. Her fierce personality paired up with her beauty was not an easy one to topple.

"Well I am a student of business studies. I'm having my masters from the University of Texas. I also wait table at North Italia and umm I live with my Grandmaa," replied Kate.

"That's a lot," Andrew squeezed his eyes and emphasized surprised. "You're right. That IS a lot but that is also what I want. I am very happy," asserted Kate.

"How come I've never seen you if you study at University of Texas," replied Andrew. "Nature had better plans maybe," smiled Kate.

"Oh that is what I am sure of," expressed Andrew.

"It's getting late. Grandmaa must be waiting for me," Kate pulled her bag close.

"Are we taking the subway?" asked Andrew getting up.

"Are you coming with me?" asked Kate, intrigued.

"Are you kidding? I am going to put in all the effort I can to win you over," Andrew said charmingly.

Kate kept changing sides that night with a big smile on her face imagining him over and over again and what it would be like to get to know him, meet him every day and maybe even feel his warmth in her arms one day.

# Chapter 2: Different as Night and Day

"When am I meeting him?" Rose said, feeding Dustie. "Soon maa!" Kate runs down the stairs.

"Oh look at you! You look so beautiful Kate. My pretty doll! He is one lucky man," exclaimed Rose joyfully.

Dustie ran and purred around Kate's legs. She was wearing a red square neck dress and had hair down. Her black curly hair matched her black heels. It had been three months since they had started dating. It was like the beginning of any relationship. Everything was perfect and exciting.

October had, as usual, betrayed the Texans of cool autumn days. The trees, however, had been up to their duty of shedding rusty leaves, making Austin look like a forest of redwoods. Kate left the house with Rose's kiss on the forehead, thrilled to see Andrew. It was a weekday, and Kate had scrapped enough time to make time for Andrew as he had to leave the city the next day.

Kate had chosen an expensive restaurant for their day together. Kate sat there waiting for Andrew. Seconds changed into minutes, and minutes changed into hours, and there was no sign of Andrew. Calls and messages went unanswered. Kate could not believe this. All her efforts had gone to vein. He had occasionally been late, but he never stood her up before. He always used to turn Kate's sadness the other way around with his charm, but this time, the chances seemed measly for him.

Kate entered Rose's room in tears. "Oh my sweet child! What happened to you?" Rose got up from her bed, putting on her glasses.

"He didn't come," Kate cried.

"What? Why?" asked Rose worriedly?

"I do not know. He won't pick up or reply me," replied Kate.

"Did you check up with any of his friends? There must be something darling. Do not be so upset. Come here," Rose hugged Kate and covered her with sheets.

Kate spent the night in Rose's bed. It was the only place she would come to when she was tired of fighting with the people around. The sky that night was full of stars, and the moon shone brightly. Seagulls squawked through the night near the dock. The frogs hooted. The crickets chirped. It seemed that the night was fully aware of the broken heart, and the creatures of the night protested against it.

The next morning Rose woke Kate up with pancakes in bed. Someone rang the bell. "Let me get that," Rose turned towards the door. Andrew was standing in the doorway. "What can I do for you?" asked Rose expressionlessly.

"I was here to see Kate. Is she awake?" asked Andrew.

"No she is not. Can I take a message?"

"Umm. Oh. I was really hoping I could talk to her. Just let her know that I'm sorry about last night. I am leaving in 30 minutes. I might not be able to reach her from there. It's a secluded area," Andrew nervously laid out.

Kate was listening from Rose's room. She went up to the door, "Maa, I'm here."

"Hey, Kate I'm really sorry. It was Bob's birthday party and I got a little bit drunk. I'm so sorry. I swear I will make it up to you," he pleaded.

"Did you get drunk when you knew you had dinner with me?" Kate said, surprised.

 "Like I said I'm really sorry. I swear, I will make it up to you," apologized Andrew. "I'm going to be gone for a long time. Can you come here? Please" Andrew made a sorry face extending his arms. Kate smiled and hugged him.

"Come here kid. I need to talk to you," asserted Rose as Kate closed the door. "Kate dear you are a mature smart woman. Is he the same?" Rose continued holding Kate's hands.

 "What do you mean maa?" asked Kate.

"Look I will be honest with you. You told me he is a graduate. Why does he not have a job? How is he supporting himself? What are his plans for his future? He does not seem…he seems very careless and living in his own world," expressed Rose. Kate looked at her bewildered. "Look baby. I just do not want you getting hurt," Rose replied worriedly.

"Maa…I know he seems a bit sloppy but he has promised me that he will figure something out soon. He takes odd jobs from and there sometimes. That is how it is working for him for now. And he loves me. He really does," replied Kate, teary-eyed.

"If you say so honey pie. If you say so," Rose hugged Kate.

The next two weeks were spent around disconnected calls and late messages. Andrew had gone hiking with some friends in the mountains. Kate spent her moons and suns worried for Andrew. The golden butterfly dodging rain bullets had seemed to be finally hit, hurting her wings, but she was stronger than this. Andrew finally came back, and Kate knew she had to remind him of his promises.

Hands in hands, the sweethearts entered a bakeshop for some doughnuts. "Hello Rue! I missed you!" Kate greeted a close friend.

"Aww I missed you more! How's is that paper on public relations effectiveness in public health institutions going on?"

"Yuck! Keep me away from that stuff," asserted Andrew putting his hands up.

Rue looked at Kate confused as Andrew picked up a sample doughnut from the counter.

"Oh I'm sorry this is Andrew. I told you about Andrew, my boyfriend. Andrew this is my friend Rue," introduced Kate smiling confusedly.

"Ah! Rue! I have heard a lot about you," replied Andrew eyeing the doughnuts.

"So what brings you here?" asked Rue uncomfortably.

"Andrew was craving doughnuts," Kate replied as Andrew walked to the end of the counter.

"I'm sorry I didn't take him as someone you would go out with," mumbled Rue.

Kate looked at Rue confused and was about to say something when Andrew came towards them, "Kate I got them. Let's go," announced Andrew.

"Oh okay. Let's go honey," replied Kate turning. "Actually my love, you have got to pay. Next treat will be on me," said Andrew.

"Yeah yeah baby," said Kate, nervously taking money out.

The minutes on Kate and Andrew's clock ran differently. The minutes ran as if in different dimensions altogether. Kate raced with the clock while Andrew would not even sit at the start line. She was an avid butterfly, and he was a dormant larva. Many times Kate tried to talk to Andrew about getting serious about his life, but he would always turn the conversation around. Kate seemed helpless at the hands of his passionate love for her. He always had a way around her.

"Andy?" asked Kate as Andrew lay with his head in her lap in his room. Andre lived with his friends in an apartment. His room was full of music posters and gross leftovers. To make it worse, his clothes were all scattered on the floor. "Yes..." replied Andrew playing with her hair.

"You know Tory from work, right?" Kate asked.

"Mhmm," Andrew continued playing with her hair.

"He told me about an opening in his department. It's of technical content manager...Can I talk to him about you?" asked Kate.

"I do not need it," Andrew got serious all of a sudden.

"Why? It's good money. You can use it," Kate asserted.

"What do you mean?" Andrew got up angrily, "Am I not good enough for you? Is that it? Is it about your friend Rue? Did you get embarrassed paying for me?"

Kate's face turned pale surprised, "Andrew...."

"What else is it Kate? I want to enjoy my life. Why are you being so selfish? Give me some time I will get you anything you want. Do not worry you would not be marrying a poor guy!" Andrew lashed out.

"What? Are you kidding me? The only reason I asked you was because I was worried for you! I can manage my own expense if you have not noticed. I want you to be independent so you do not have to be dependent on anybody. So you can secure your future. You are hardly making it through," replied Kate.

"I am so sorry Kate that I cannot take you to fancy restaurants or give you expensive gifts. My love is all I have. Too bad that's not enough for you!" Andrew rushed out the door.

"No...Andrew!" she mumbled.

Kate stood there in a trance, "What had just happened?"

Andrew had been kicking everything on his way out of the apartment. If he would be honest, he did not want responsibilities. He just wanted to savor life in any way he could. He did not want worries sucking the happiness out of life. He wanted to be bothered by nothing. He had found love, but that was all he wanted from his life.

On Kate's way from work, she entered the subway, and it was quieter than usual. Everyone was sitting with their heads down. She held her bag cautiously and sat down. After a minute, the whole compartment sat up singing romantically. Andrew put away his disguise and emerged from the crowd singing. He had a bouquet in his hand. Kate was astonished.

Andrew put his arms around Kate, singing, "When you put your arms me, you let me know there's nothing in this world I can't do," Kate was still confused but had a smile on her face. "I am sorry Kate. I am madly in love with you. I am sorry, I lashed out on you. Let me mend my mistakes," Andrew expressed. And so, Andrew had found his way out of it again.

Andrew convinced Kate that he would have a serious job in a couple of months as first he wanted to return a favor to a friend by doing some odd jobs for him. That was a good excuse to get Kate off his back for some time.

Like Kate, Austin had gone through some ups and downs. The chilly days had taken over. Even though they knew their command would be short-termed, they tried to give Austin the best of the chilly days it had had in a while. The clouds laid a blanket of white snow. Children followed ice crystals around as they bopped on their little noses. Austin snuggled in the white blanket as long as it could before the Sun came out of its slumber party.

"Andy I know…but I cannot talk to you now. I'll stop by your apartment before I go home. My boss has already warned me two times while talking to you. Come on. Understand please. Okay I'll see you," Kate talked over the phone worriedly.

An hour passed, and Kate heard some commotion behind her. She got out of her cubicle, and she saw Andrew coming in with flowers and chocolates singing. "Katie! I missed you. I could not wait any longer, so I came here myself," exclaimed Andrew joyously. Kate led Andrew to her cubicle nervously as everybody eyed them. "Do you like the flowers?" asked Andrew.

"Keep it down, Andrew!"' Kate mumbled, tensed.

"Why what happened? Do you not like the flowers?" asked Andrew.

"No…no, it's not about the flowers. How do I put this? Okay. Andy, I love you, but you cannot barge in here like this. It is my office," Kate put words together.

"I thought it would be fun. It's okay. I'll go wait at my place for you," replied Andrew.

Kate held his face in her hands, "Andy love are you sure it's okay with you? I am so sorry. I hope you understand. I will try to get off work early. How's that?"

Kate's thoughts were all over the place, walking to Andrew's home. She was exhausted and tired, not from the stress on her body but the stress on her mind. "Andrew would never be able to grow and mature until he learns to take care of himself," she thought to herself. For now, she went on to take care of the kid she wished to turn into a man.

Tiny rain droplets ended their sky-high journey on Andrew's window inside, which Kate pampered him through the night. It was the first time she had claimed to be in love, but she did not really know what love was supposed to feel like. All she knew was that she felt safe in his arms. As for him, he was sure that what they had was pure love. Nothing else seemed to be more important in life, but that was the problem.

"Rise and shine big boy!" exclaimed Kate as Andrew came out of the room. Kate was standing in the kitchen making pancakes. Andrew kissed her forehead and opened the refrigerator.

"Oh! My fridge looks different," said Andrew looking at the compartments filled with vegetables, fruits, eggs, milk, and drinks.

"Yeah. I did a grocery run. Thought you could use some food," teased Kate smiling, "The fridge is for food, you know."

"Now that's wrong. I had some expired leftovers and a pack of beers in it," laughed Andrew.

"Ha Ha, how very funny," replied Kate putting pancakes on the plates.

"Since we're on the topic, when are you going to take that job?" asked Kate nervously. "First of all, no, we are not on the topic and secondly, soon," Andrew replied, hugging Kate from the back.

"Soon?" replied Kate worriedly.

"Soon baby," assured Andrew and tickled Kate.

"Oh Andy, love. You are coming with me on Tina's birthday party right?" asked Kate, munching.

"At your service my queen," replied Andrew,

"Oh. I do not need to bring a present for her. Do I?"

"I'll take care of it," Kate touched his nose affectionately.

The area by the swimming pool was decorated with balloons and fairy lights hanging from trees. Exquisite flowers were arranged on all the tables. A strawberry cheesecake saying "Happy Birthday Tina" was surrounded by flowers. Jazz music was on, and people were sipping on their drinks talking. "Hello!" Kate greeted Tina warmly, "What a beautiful, party!"

"Isn't it? Rue arranged it all!" expressed Tina.

"Hi Tina. A very Happy birthday, "congratulated Andrew,"

"Thank you, Andrew!" replied Tina joyously, pulling Kate's hand, "Let me show you something."

While the girls gossiped together, Andrew gulped cocktails. To Kate's surprise, when she got back, Andrew was smashed. Kate held her purse in one hand and Andrew in the other. The birthday girl was about to cut her cake, so her father raised a toast to her, "I cannot begin to explain how proud I am of my daughter. She is a wonderful human being, so kind and generous. She started her journey from the very bottom. Now she is the Sales Marketing Head of her company. I am so proud of you my baby!"

"No no no," Andrew spoke up drunkenly. Kate held his arm, but he jerked it away, "What is that life to be proud of? She is deliberately chopping her head off with all those responsibilities and worries and you are proud of her? You all live a disgusting life. Sorry not sorry,"

Everyone got surprised. Kate was both surprised and embarrassed.

"Excuse me? I love my life. I am living my dreams!" replied Tina angrily.

Andrew scoffed, "Yeah sure!"

"What do you mean? Do we all give up our jobs and live on the streets? Who pays your bills?" yelled Tina.

"She does," Andrew pointed at Kate, "I live my life like it's meant to be lived. Carefree. Like a bird."

"Enough with this Andrew," Kate pulled him away angrily and dragged him away from the party. She got him in the car and dropped a passed-out Andrew to his apartment. She stood there looking at him, "Were they really meant to be together? Does he feel this strongly about life?"

A lot of questions stormed in Kate's head. It had been a year since Kate had drowned in Andrew's love, but it had also been a year since she had been trying to understand him and still could not how more time and energy was demanded of her in this relationship. Tears trickled down by her exhaustion and humiliation. There was no validation of her feelings that day by nature. The night was quiet as though numbed by the pain.

Kate avoided Andrew for the next few days. She did not have the courage to blend the two distant worlds.

"She's there," Rue pointed out to Kate as she entered the bakeshop. Tina was sitting on one of the tables. Kate turned towards her after taking a deep breath.

"Hey," Kate mumbled. "Hey Kate. How are you?" replied Tina sincerely. "I'm good. Look I wanted to apologize for your birthday. Andrew was way out of his league and he is really sorry about it," Kate lied.

"Is he?" Tina looked in her eyes and leaned forward, holding her hands, "Look Kate, you are a smart person. I do not know how you do not see this. He does not match with you. You are polar opposites. And it's not just me. Everybody thinks that."

"I know. We're different. I get that," mumbled Kate, "but I love him and he loves me. I want things to work."

"I know you will figure it out on your own. It is just that you were the one who pushed me to be independent. Before you, I was just dependent on my dad for everything. The financial dependency suffocates you. I have felt the change. I would not have been here if it was not for you. Now I just cannot believe that someone so oblivious of the realities of life is your boyfriend. How does he plan on spending his life? He cannot depend on you forever. That is unfair to you. He must be capable of so much than he is allowing himself explore," expressed Tina.

Kate did not need anybody to tell her the truth, for she knew all of it. The man she loved was determined to throw his life away. He was giving his life away in the hands of others because he was not willing to take care of it himself. It was up to others to keep it safe like a fragile diamond on their neck or crush it like a bug under their feet.

# Chapter 3: Beautiful Deceiving Love

Kate's eyes followed the naughty little creatures, kids, running around with their tiny feet and pulling each other's legs as she sat in the park. Sometimes she would come here on the weekends to look at the sunset. That time of the evening never seemed to betray her of happiness. The giggles of the children playing around on the swings as the day surrendered itself to darkness were a reminder that life is worth living.

Kate looked over at Andrew coming towards her, holding ice cones as the pleasant August wind blew through her hair. Andrew had done everything Kate had asked her to turn his life around. He had taken a job at her office and had promised to look at life maturely. Kate had nothing against his wild-spirited nature. All she wanted was for him to take charge of it so he did not get dragged away with it. In this world, everyone should learn to take care of themselves. Every being is destined to play its part in the cycle of the universe.

"Hey," Andrew said, sliding on the bench with Kate. Kate took the ice cream smiling. "It's beautiful, isn't it?" expressed Andrew as he looked at the sun setting. "It is. Magnificent, it is," replied Kate.

"So how's your job going at the office?" asked Kate. "It's good. It's good," replied Andrew. "I am sorry baby that my exams clashed with your first month of the job," expressed Kate. "Hey. It's okay. You will be at the office in just three more days and then we can spend our lunch breaks together every day," replied Andrew smiling, putting her head on his shoulder. It was after so many months that Kate's heart had been at peace. Everything was perfect.

"No you cannot have my fries. No!" Andrew glided his lunch away teasingly. "Why? You can have my share if you want!" expressed Kate eyeing the fries. "Cow food? No thanks. I'm good," chuckled Andrew. "Ah. You are so mean. It is a healthy salad!" replied Kate. "Yeah then why don't you eat it?" giggled Andrew.

Tory passed through Kate's cubicle, looking awkwardly. "Oh hi Tory!" exclaimed Kate, but Tory did not turn back. "Okay that was weird," Kate sounded confused. Andrew looked a bit nervous and said, faking confidence, "If you ask me, the whole guy is weird," "I do not know him very well but he was so nice when he told me about the job opening for you in his department," Kate replied. "No Kate. He's so rude to everybody in our apartment. He lies around and loves to see other fight. Seriously he is the worst," asserted Andrew. "Huh," replied Kate unbelievingly.

Kate won herself the employee of the year award. Her hard work and diligence showed through her work both at the office and the university. Soon enough, she started saving money to buy a small car wash company she had an eye for. Rose was so ecstatic to see Kate grow and accomplish her dreams, but just then, something happened to put Kate through a miserable chapter once again.

Kate was working away from the wheel when Tory came to her quite agitated. "Hi Tory. What's the matter you seem tense," asked Kate worriedly. "Kate look you know I helped you with Andrew with this job and you also know I am his supervisor," expressed Tory. "Oh I…I was not aware of that. What happened?" Kate replied anxiously. "Yeah well, he has been driving me crazy. That day, I came to tell you but he was with you. Look Kate! I was only doing this as a favor to you but I cannot keep this from the boss anymore," replied Tory angrily.

"What is it? Tell me that!" asked Kate. "He comes in late every day. He does not even get half the work I ask him to do in a day. All the time he is on his phone. He takes breaks whenever he wants. Sometimes, he is gone for two to three hours Kate. He does not listen. It is like he has no ears!" uttered Tory furiously.

It was like somebody had switched Kate off. Now she understood why Andrew was bad-mouthing Tory that day. He did not want her to believe Tory. She looked at him for a good one minute without saying anything. "Do not stand in the way of him and the boss," mumbled Kate numbly, "Let him deal with Andrew. Step aside."

Kate's relationship with Andrew was a rollercoaster. Just when she thought she had caught a break, the downhill hit made her heart skip a beat. As she exited the building, she saw Andrew sitting with a box of his belongings. He got up seeing Kate. Kate went up to her. "They fired me Kate. I'm sorry. I tried," Andrew mumbled. "I know. Torry told me why they could," Kate replied.

"I cannot believe Tory came to you. He is the one behind this all. I hate that man. I want to punch him," said Andrew madly. "Andrew, Tory did not fire you. The boss did and he is not so stupid to fire you just because someone said so," replied Kate slowly. "Oh Kate!" Andrew expressed his frustration.

"I'm just coming back from boss's office Andrew. I really wanted to give you the benefit of doubt but I should not have. I thought you had changed," replied Kate, "We are too different Andrew. I wish you well. I hope you realize that I wanted this for your own good. Someday when it will hit you hard, you might get it. Do not be so foolish to put yourself at the mercy of others. Life will treat you cruelly," mumbled Kate emotionally and walked away.

Kate distanced herself from Andrew for the next four months. She cut him off from everywhere. Her heart felt like it was caught in a barb-wire tightening slowly, but she had to stay there for not to let her cross the fence with him.

Rose had been her guardian angel from the time she was born, but it also made her realize that if she had not been on her feet, she could not have taken Kate in, and she would have been juggled up between foster homes. The people who brought Kate into this world and were supposed to love her the most had abandoned her. If Kate did not build herself, she could not be there for Rose in her old age, and the sad truth was Kate could be in place of Rose in a few decades. This was how important being financially stable she thought was. Everything else and everyone else in life can tremble and fall apart, but you are what you will have forever, so why would you not invest in that.

Life is an incredibly meaningful journey. It is not meant to be wasted lying around. It is for one to look inside and grow from within.

"Maa, your lunch and dinner are in the fridge in case I get late. Are you sure you do not want me to call Nancy?" Kate kissed Rose on the cheek as she lay down, hiding under the covers. "Oh you worry too much. This fever will be gone even before you come. Hush now," Rose grumbled. "It better be, okay?" giggled Kate.

Kate picked up her bag and opened the door. Her smile faded away. She felt her hands losing their grip on her bag. There were flowers in the doorway with a note on them. She knew right away who they were from. It had been a lot of time since Andrew had stopped reaching out to Kate, and she thought that he had walked his own way.

"You might be thinking why I am leaving these flowers at your doorstep today. The truth is you never left my mind. Only I know how I have stopped myself from coming to you these past months, but I wanted to be worthy of you when I met you again. I certainly was not before. Can I have one last chance? If your answer is yes, can we please meet at "Roaring Fork" at 8:00 P.M.?

I love you." read the note.

Kate's blood got cold, and she felt the need to sit down. All of the trouble and energy she had gone through to put this behind her began knocking at her already bloody door again. But what if she could walk the burning bridge to the other side where the pacifying snow could tend to her blazing wounds.

If one had to make a choice of his poison, he should know the game of "what ifs" is the deadliest.

When the mind and heart fight the battle of "what ifs," the heart usually cheats its way to the win.

The whole day Kate's mind remained preoccupied with the idea of a life with Andrew. Sitting on the bed, she looked outside the window. The seagulls fighting over their share of food squawked in the February sky filled with clouds ready to dominate the city in white.

Kate got up to match the city. Dressed in all white, she soothed her aching heart. She wore the bracelet Andrew had given her but then put it away after a minute. She had to be realistic. It was today against her future. The wishful past had nothing to do with it.

"Honey? Be careful," Rose asserted worriedly. "Yeah maa," replied Kate.

Kate found herself standing under the bug wooden signboard spelling "Roaring Fork." It was one of the fanciest restaurants in the area. Kate looked at her watch, and it was 7:50 P.M. She sighed, knowing there was no way Andrew could be here before at least 30 minutes. A minute had passed, and a waiter came to her asking if she was waiting for somebody. "Yes I am but he's not here yet," replied Kate confidently. "Are you sure? There's a gentleman under the name Tales waiting inside. Would you like me to check for you?" replied the waiter. "Um. No. I will check myself," replied Kate, still in disbelief.

"It must be another Tales but what a coincidence it would be," she thought, walking by the clinking of glasses and clatter of the forks against the plates. The waiter walked her to an outside dining area overlooking a lake surrounded by trees. She saw Andrew from a distance, but the waiter had to guide her all the way through because she could not believe her eyes.

Andrew was looking at the lake wearing a suit, and his hair was brushed through, and most surprisingly, he was there before time. Hiding her stunning look, she sat in front of Andrew. Andrew's face brimmed with joy and nervousness. She had never seen him like this way before.

"How are you Kate?" smiled Andrew. "I'm good. I'm good. You look good too. Very good," replied Kate, confused. "It's all because of you," replied Andrew. "How so?" asked Kate. "I have a job in a prestigious company, all thanks to you," expressed Andrew. "Oh. Congratulations," replied Kate. Andrew held her hand and said, "Look Kate, I was an idiot. A very big idiot, in fact. I now understand what you mean. I am living well. The company has given me a car. I have a good salary. I do not have to ask for favors from anybody now. I um… I am out of that sorry excuse for an apartment. Yeah! It feels so freeing," expressed Andrew passionately. Kate could not hide her stunned face anymore. It was too much to take on. "I want to do something with my life you know. I want to quit messing around. You know, I have always had a thing for antiques. There's an antique store near my old apartment. I am thinking to invest there," continued Andrew.

"Um I do not know what to say Andrew. That's an awful lot of changing in four months," replied Kate skeptically.

"I know, it may seem a lot but this is just my way of proving to you how much you mean to me and how much I want to be with you. Not just that I understand you wanted it for my sake and not yours. Please. Come back to me. There's no reason left for us not to be together," he beseeched.

Kate's heart melted once again. All the wounds she had seemed to have healed. "I missed you so much," tears trickled down her cheeks. "Hey hey I am here. I am here now. I won't go away anywhere no. no," Andrew got up and sat on the floor, holding her hands.

Their desserts seemed sweeter than usual as they were shared with love. As they walked outside, Andrew asked her, "Can I drop you?"

"I would love for you to but," Kate got interrupted.

"But you came in your own car," said Andrew looking at her car keys. "Well then want to race?" asked Andrew, smiling.

Kate looked at him deceivingly and then ran to her car.

Andrew followed suit, laughing, "You are such a cheater!"

Kate had not felt so much good in a long time. She came home with flushing cheeks, and it was not because of the cold. Dustie surprisingly came to her purring against her leg. Dustie seemed to have to hat Kate as showed her affection to Grace once in a blue moon. Everything seemed to be in place once again. Kate would not have anything way another way.

The next weeks were just beautiful. Every other day the couple would snuggle up in each other's hug to watch a movie at Andrew's new place. It was a spacious studio apartment that Andrew had adored with Kate's favorite flowers, lilies.

Kate had her birthday on the 27th of April. Andrew planned a surprise for her.

"Kate I thought I would not need to call you but my fever is spiking through the roof. Can you please come home early today?" mumbled Rose sickly.

Kate hurriedly left her class as Rose had never called her like this before. She entered home with heavy breathing and rushed to Rose's room.

"Surprise!" shouted Rose, Andrew, and her friends. The room was adorned with flowers and balloons. Everybody sang her happy birthday.

Kate covered her face, amazed. "Hey…thank you!" said Kate as Andrew came forward to hug her. Kate then moved towards Rose, "Do not you dare scare me like that again."

The appetizing smell of the different types of cakes and baked goods served with tea left the house with a tempting aroma. Kate cut the cake as everyone clapped and sang for her. She opened presents for everybody.

Just when Kate thought it was an end to a delightful evening, Andrew invited her to his car. "Where are you taking me?" asked Kate curiously. "You will see," replied Andrew smiling as they sped away into the sunset.

Andrew brought her to his apartment. When he opened the door, Kate was out of words to see the floor was covered with lilies, and candles were lit throughout the apartment. Balloons were hung from the ceiling.

"Andrew!" sparked Kate in joy.

"Do you like it?" asked Andrew holding her by the waist.

"O my God I love it! When did you do all this? It's breathtaking," Kate looked around.

"Come here. Time for your present," asserted Andrew holding her arm.

"Andrew. You did not have to…." Kate sincerely replied.

There was a big box on the bed with a bow on it. Kate opened it, and it was an exquisite red skirt which she had passed by one day and liked.

"No! You remembered?" Kate gasped in joy. "Thank you so much baby for such an amazing day. I could not even have ever dreamt of it but baby you should not have. This is all too much. You have just started your job. You should be spending on 'You.'"

"What is the difference between me and you? It is the same for me," replied Andrew, "and besides you did so much for me. It is time for me to do the same for you."

With that, Andrew kissed her cheek, and it warmed her heart as she thought she had found her soul mate.

The never-ending summer in Austin had reached August. The parched soil begged for rain, but the Sun had to shine in its glory for some more time. The birds hovered over the Colorado River throughout the day to quench their thirst.

Kate drove up to Andrew's apartment to surprise him. She had been planning to do so for some time, but somehow Andrew was always with her. Kate got out of the elevator and saw two tall and sturdy strange men leave the apartment. She stuck to the wall suddenly and got back inside the elevator again. The men joined her.

Kate called Andrew as soon as she got in the car, "Andrew? Where are you? I just saw two very strange men leave out of your apartment,"

"What strange men?" asked Andrew worriedly.

"Well two bald dangerous looking men!" replied Kate scared.

"Oh! Oh you must be talking about Ben and Harold!" asserted Andrew nervously, "Oh babe you had me worried there for a moment. What were you doing at my apartment at this time? I told you I would be Joshua. Remember?"

"Oh I must have forgotten. Anyway I'm heading home," replied Kate confused.

Andrew was clearly hiding something but what people say is true, "Love is blind." Kate could not see through a façade Andrew had set up in front of her eyes, but what the façade was, she had yet to find. Mother Earth teaches us lessons, and the lessons learned the hard way are the ones we stick to. Kate was just about to have her hard lesson. For now, she obliviously drove home on the beguilingly beautiful road, love had conjured for her.

# Chapter 4: Gasping for Air in Love

"Andy? Why do you have only two formals hanging here? Don't tell me you have been juggling between these two shirts in the office from all these months," exclaimed Kate surprisingly as she opened Andrew's cupboard.

"No! They are at the dry cleaners'. Though I do need more shirts. You will help me shop, right," Andrew kissed Kate's forehead handing her coffee. "Oh yes! Let's go now!" replied Kate joyously.

"No no. Not now. Maybe a couple of days later," replied Andrew sipping coffee. "Why? Are you short on money? Baby you know you can always count on me. Do you need money?" asked Kate.

"No no. I'm good. How's the coffee?" asked Andrew. "Eghh how much sugar did you put in it!" asserted Kate disgustingly, tasting the coffee.

"Oh I forgot you like it bitter like yourself. I like it sweet like myself," teased Andrew. Kate put her mug down and hassled with him. The apartment echoed with their laughter.

The doorbell rang. Andrew got up and received a package. "What is it?" asked Kate.

"Oh nothing it is for a friend," mumbled Andrew and went into the bathroom.

"Okay I'm going to head out. It's 12 already," said Kate getting up. As she was about to exit the door, she noticed the name on the package was not Andrew's. It was for a "James Taylor." The address was listed as James Taylor's.

Kate thought of it to be strange and thought that she would ask Andrew about it, but unfortunately, she forgot to mention it again.

The cycle of the months had given February a chance to shine again though it failed to meet the expectations of the Texans. Their excitement for the already meagre winter months faded away with a not-so-cold February, but the birds and animals were happy. Summer was their time to play out.

Kate checked her voicemail while leaving the office. "Kate, I am going with some friends for hiking. I am sorry for not telling you in advance. We just made the plan. I love you and I will miss you. I will try to maintain contact with you, okay? Do not worry. Bye," the phone beeped for Andrew's message.

It was very strange. Andrew had not gone hiking since the first time they met, and it was very weird for him to just drop a voicemail and go away. It was not like him. Nevertheless, Kate managed to talk to him every day, and he told her how his friends dragged him with them.

Three days later, Kate stopped at a gas station. As she was filling up on gas, she saw a man inside the mart that looked like Andrew. She went inside, and to her surprise, it was Andrew.

"Andrew? What in the world are you doing here?" asked Kate furiously and confused. When she got a good look at Andrew, she realized his face was covered in bruises. Andrew was as shocked as she was to see him.

"What is this Andrew? What happened to your face? What is this?" asked Kate taking off his hoodie. "Okay. Come outside. Come…please," Andrew requested her to come out.

"What is this Andrew?" asked Kate once again while going out. "I didn't tell you about it because I did not want you to get mad at me. I did not want you to see me like this…look I'm really sorry," replied Andrew with a black eye.

"Who did this to you and why?" Kate wanted answers.

"I got in a fight. It was a stupid bar fight. I did not want you think I'm going back to my habits. Please try to understand," explained Andrew.

"Andrew… I'll see you in sometime. Right now I'm so angry. I don't want to say anything I'll regret later," said Kate and drove away.

The warm-chilly wind on Kate's face matched the mixed emotions she was feeling. She was angry, and she was distant from herself. All the past flashes came to her. Had she pushed herself in the burning lava again? How many times has she had fell for him over and over again?

The pillows did not feel soft on her cheeks as she hit the bed that night. Dustie climbed up the stairs and curled up with her. Kate closed her eyes and prayed the next day brought some sanity her way.

Kate numbed herself down. She met with Andrew but was not the same as before. Her soul had been lost somewhere inside her.

"Kate?" Andrew shook Kate somewhere in her own world. 'Yeah yeah! I am here," replied Kate adjusting herself. "Are you okay?" asked Andrew, concerned.

"Yeah I am fine. What were you saying?" asked Kate. "Um. I was saying Joshua' mother is having a surgery for her cancer and he was short for some money. He asked me but I do not have that kind of money. Can you pitch in?" expressed Andrew.

"How much do you need from me?" asked Kate. "2000," mumbled Andrew. "2000 dollars?" Kate got surprised. "Yeah I told you it is for a surgery. It is expensive. Imagine the load on Joshua's shoulders," Andrew replied.

"Look Andrew 2000 is a lot of money...," said Kate.

"I know; I know but he promises to pay you back as soon as he can. Come on, I do not want to say 'no' to him," requested Andrew.

"Okay," replied Kate.

"Okay?" asked Andrew joyously. "Okay but I will give Joshua the money myself," asserted Kate doubtfully.

"Okay I see what is going on. You do not trust me. You think, I am lying to you!" Andrew got hyper and stood up.

"Tell me that has not happened before," Kate asserted loudly, still sitting.

"Do not rub that in my face Kate. You would only point out the things where I messed up and never appreciate the things I did good," ragged Andrew, "I have changed so much for you. I have done so much for you but we do not talk about that."

"You changed for me? How many times do I have to say it Andrew? I wanted you to change for "YOU" so "YOU" can have a good life. So "YOU" can hold your head high. YOU not ME!" Kate argued.

"Okay you do not trust me. You think that I am lying. You want to give the money to Joshua? You give it to Joshua!" exclaimed Andrew and went outside.

Kate sat down and broke into tears. She never thought she would have to get defensive with Andrew. She was in pieces, and the man whom she loved was the one behind it.

A few days later, Kate went to Andrew's home with the money. She was mad at Andrew but still was worried for the needy Joshua.

As she entered, she saw the same strange men in the apartment. "There is your princess with the money!" yelled one of the men. Andrew was sitting on the sofa, terrified." Why are these men again in your apartment again, Andrew?" Kate took out the money scared. "Do not worry. We are just here for our money, and by the way, it is not his apartment." one of the men said and took the money from her hands. "What? What are these men saying? asked Kate, scared.

"You mind telling her?" one of the men said as he counted the money. "They my friends. They let me stay here until they came back in the city," mumbled Andrew embarrassed.

"But the apartment and the car are privileges of your job. What are you saying?" replied Kate in disbelief. "Him and a job?" the men looked at each other and laughed.

"Lady if he had a job I do not think you would be giving his owed money? And we are leaving with the car. That is not his too btw. Good luck," asserted one of the men and went out the door.

Kate stood there in a puddle of her tears. It was like somebody had stabbed her right through the heart. She did not wish a betrayal so bad on somebody.

"Kate Kate!" Andrew got up and held Kate. "Do not you dare touch me!" mumbled Kate.

"Kate I did all of it for you!" explained Andrew crying.

"Does it not show you the lengths I will go to because I love you?" continued Andrew.

"No, Andrew. It shows me the lengths you will go to avoid being a man. It shows me you will do anything in this world but be sincere with yourself and ultimately with others.

You know what, everybody told me we were not for each other, but I believed in you. I did it. I do not know why I thought you could grow and mature. You are still stuck where I found you.

Do you see how much mess you have created because of your stubbornness? The free life you wanted has you sitting at the feet of others begging. You will soon run out of friends because nobody can take care of a person who is not willing to take care of himself. You are no far away from being homeless, Andrew. When you have to fight for every bite, you take you will know.

Look what you did to me. I was your friend. I was your lover. You swore by me. Look what you did to me. Look what you did to yourself.

I tried Andrew. I really did in spite of what everybody said. Now you are at the mercy of this world, "cried Kate.

"Are you just going to leave me alone now Kate? Cannot you stay for the sake of love we had for THREE years?" asked Andrew, weeping.

"Shit happens in life Andrew but this time you and you alone are responsible for it," replied Kate leaving.

Andrew had used up all his chances with Kate. Even he knew that the hurt he had caused her was irreversible. He sat there collecting the pieces of his broken heart. It was time to put down the gun he had used for it and take a step towards the light.

It took him years and years to bounce back from the living hell he had created for himself. It was a road full of thorns on which he had to walk barefoot. He could understand then that laziness and lying around would have never served him or the people he loved anything. He wanted life to be fair to him when he was not fair to himself.

Kate had left his life for good but as said before, Mother Earth teaches us hard lessons to make us stick to them, and this was Andrew's hard lesson. He had to be his own before he could be anybody else's.

Life is a precious gift that needs to be cherished and appreciated. If we take ourselves for granted, so will others. Even the most powerful of emotions, "love", cannot save you until and unless first it is directed from "you" towards "you." You might think the consequences of carelessness, lying, and deceiving fall on anyone but you. However, you are the one who gets hit by the thunder the most as you lie in the ashes of your world.

Life is what you make it.

You are who you make yourself.

If you like this story and the concept behind it, please leave a review on Amazon!

I hope you had fun in the world of imagination!